252

Caelum Sky Illustrated #1
Worlds Apart

By

Andrea Radeck

ISBN- 10: 099070341X
ISBN- 13: 978-0-9907034-1-9
Library of Congress Control Number: 2014915843

Dedicated
to
Hilda & Hank Riemer

1

The first thing I heard, ever, was a grunt.

A snort of some sort - that's what woke me up.

Like someone clearing the back of their throat - too lazy to put any real effort into it - the sound was so repulsive that I couldn't help but take notice. Which is disappointing, retrospectively: it could've been something interesting like the slow, wailing howl of the far depths of Hell or the indistinguishable rumbling of beasts and creatures never-before-classified - or screams! Scary things, frightening things, *any* things.

But no, nothing unique like that, just a grunt that startled me a little.

I opened my eyes - figuratively. My eyes were plenty open already. Consciousness set me adrift staring at the slats in someone's ribcage, jiggling around in front of me like a macabre Halloween prop. When I realized that this wasn't actually a decoration, that the bones and vertebrae were physically connected and moving about, it became pretty clear I wasn't okay.

I shuddered with a dose of surprise as bones closer to my view suddenly shifted back - my eyes instantly locked to them. There quivered a pair of arm bones connected to my wrist bones, 'hands' locked tightly to a pair of handcuffs linked to the 'people' both in front of and behind me in one giant chain. It drifted through their backs; their ribcages tapered off to just vertebrae before fading out to nothing at all. The tiniest bit more concerned for my situation, I saw that I suffered the same fate.

Something screeched in my ear as a loose, leathery wing nearly scraped the top of my head. The creature gave a sort of unnecessary bob to its flight; dull, lifeless eyes rolling about in its head while the beast charged up the side of what appeared to be a massive cavern. My eyes lingered for a second before slowly crawling up the walls of this hellish pit, really getting a sense of how big this place was. Half-wrecked pillars propped the ceiling of the cavern up, detail faded nearly everywhere. Lines and lines of skele-folk wandered though cut archways, patrolled by these dopey-eyed demons lazily flapping about.

Farther down, the mist grew thicker, with lines of people crossing endless rooms down a chasm headed to the center of the earth. Something swam among them, large and dark, its body meticulously black. Its green, soulless green eyes glided behind a pillar and out of view, curling around the adjoining room and watching its surroundings carefully. The sight of the beast sealed any lingering doubts that this wasn't Hell, that my very real death hadn't taken place, and that I wasn't in the depths of a nightmare.

I had no memories of my life, aside from very basic things that even babies know: eating and sleeping, day and night; life in general; going to the movies alone was embarrassing, and culture defined who we were. But as for a personal life, I drew a blank. I had no memories of myself, no ideas where I might've lived, how I'd lived my life, if I had kids, or if I'd nursed sick cats back to health for a living. The only thing I did remember - a tiny blip of a memory - was a pair of blue eyes. They owned no body; there was no face with them, just a pair of godforsaken eyes staring at me from the side, bugged-out and terrified.

I had no idea where they came from, if they were my own or belonged to someone else. They were just there, rolling in my head as I tilted this way and that. The rest of my mind was sickeningly clean. I had no idea of anything: what I truly looked like, how old I was before I died or what gender I was - I didn't even have a name! I owned nothing but a hundred and forty bones (give or take). The handcuffs were probably rented.

I was Me, and that's all I knew. Me… and those eyes.

Pulled about as if on some motorized walkway, I tried saying something, to maybe try and give a quick "howdy" to the demons screeching around. Nothing. My skeletal jawbone snapped back into place, clicking my teeth together as I just floated past instead. Realizing that at least I could hear, I clicked to a beat and sort of looked around like a bored child. Behind me was uniform: each skele-folk kept their glare straight ahead, wrists out and stiff as ever. When I looked to the other lines, they were the same - I seemed to be the only one moving around.

Something darted beneath my vertebrae, swimming to the next pillar and leaving just a few cenepedial legs showing, face locked onto someone else. Peering over, trying to see just what this thing was, I suddenly bumped into the neighbor behind me, and then into his friend behind him. Like slowly falling down a pair of horizontal stairs, I tumbled out of position; frightened, arms flailing, and hit by each successive skele-half behind me.

Scrambling to get a grip on something or someone beneath me, I shoved myself away from the line. They all passed by at the same pace, skulls still facing forward as my spot marched farther and farther away. Frantically, I looked down at my wrists, back to the spot, then back to the rest of these loose-faced demons flapping around. One made a half-assed beep at me before flying off, continuing on his path. No big alarm. No one seemed really worried, no one cared - nothing happened. All they seemed to do was lazily move out of the way, giving me a wide berth, and continue with their jobs. I half-expected to fight my way out of there, snatch a pair of their wings and flap my way to an exit.

Chest bones quickly rising and falling like I had to catch my breath, something changed direction beneath me. The massive black something-or-other shot directly under my last dangling spine-bit as it wheeled around like a little helicopter, hundreds of claws and hands gripping onto the nearest pillar a ways down. Frozen, holding my not-breath, I saw its beady green eyes snap suddenly upwards and focus on me, narrowing. Hele-spine stopped.

"No... no, no!" I clicked. The gape of its maw lit up neon green, mouth extending farther and farther back like it was crudely stitched together. The green lights dotted the cave, back end of the monster lighting up places I couldn't see before. In a flash, it darted to the next pillar, higher up, eyes still on me. My fictitious blood went cold.

"NO! Nonononononono!" My jaws clicked furiously together as I struggled to swim, arms wheeling around like a paddleboat, trying to get away. The creature let out a snarl, crashing from pillar to pillar as if it were drunk, barely coordinating itself. Spinning my hele-spine as fast as I could, I drifted at the pace of a fast walk, scrambling for the top. I didn't know where I was going or where I could even hide from something this big. Frustrated, I changed tactics, scooping at the air as fast as I could to move the tiniest bit faster. I kept gazing back and seeing that monster lurching forward, filling more and more of my field of vision.

The air suddenly rang around me as the demon howled, crashing into the nearest pillar. Large chunks of Hell dropped from the ceiling and I was sure it'd be crushed, offering me a fair chance to at least gain some distance. I expected some sort of satisfying crunch, but the ceiling only dropped a few inches before slowly healing itself back to the top, solidifying once again as the monster perched there, trying to find me with its impressively tiny eyes. I huffed though my collarbones.

"Aww, come on!" I cried through nonexistent lips, apparently so fond of talking that I was going to keep on doing it, despite that no one could possibly hear me and I certainly wasn't saying anything.

The demon located me again, gnashing its teeth as the green mist seeped everywhere. Like some hopeless idiot, I kept swimming away, making absolutely no difference in my chance of escape. I guess I just didn't want to drift there and give up so easily. I'd rather hang on to an impossible wager than keel lightly to the side, disappointed with myself. This was my barely counting, hardly-human life!

Its mouth stretched wider, secondary and tertiary mouths opening from various other places on the beast. With my head pretty much facing backwards,

each arm swinging around as fast as my little shoulders would allow, the creature launched from that last pillar. It took about half a second of motion for it to catch up, mouth opening wider and wider as the two of us were pointed vertically.

This wasn't fair! Here I was, stuck being some sort of soul-snack for a giant, pissed off demon crocodile centipede - that's what my life totaled to. Other people could become musicians, doctors, accountants - anything - and the best I'd be known for was some stupid skeleton half that got so pathetically nowhere that the demon didn't even have to try hard. Even in the four-and-a-half minutes I'd been awake, I knew that was pretty screwed up.

With a sudden rush of adrenaline, the monster sped up, using every bit of its power to snap onto those very last links of spine, my arms suddenly pinned down by my sides as I rocketed around the cavern at a breakneck speed. Clicking in silent, petrified screams, I saw the demon crash into the next wall, senses dislodged for a second as we started shooting to the other side. Hell seemed almost small. Thrown about, the pressure suddenly dropped from my bones, I spun, barely conscious and alone. Swinging my head around, trying to understand what had just happened, I realized that the demon was playing with its food. I could see it take a victory lap to the side, zipping about like a bolt as it shot to the bottom of the pit, eyes still keen on me and giving me a few seconds to mill over my long, fulfilling life.

"D... daammit... "I spun, just aware enough to realize what was about to happen, but not conscious enough to say anything or think anything important. Distantly, that beast screeched, charging forward as fast as it could go. "H... hate this world. Hate you... stupid looking... demons."

I tried pointing at the lazily flapping demon closest to me and realized that I didn't even have any arm bones left. Whimpering pitifully, I tried to sob without tear ducts. My body slowly rotated so I could face back down and watch my own death come up to meet me.

It darted from side to side, straight from the ground and bathed bathed the caverns in an awful, puke-yellowish green light. Details faded out like I was about to get hit by a speeding train. All I could do was float there and watch it happen, whining and moaning that life was terribly unfair. The demon pushed off that last pillar, tiny eyes frenzied and nearly split open like a demonic banana. I suddenly got mad. It wasn't enough to just *think* this was bullshit, it *was* bullshit. Why did my life have to be trivialized down to the first bad decision I made? What was I supposed to do, sit and stare like some brain-dead monkey as Hell carted me along the scenic tour?

"C'mon!" I clicked silently at the nuisance, more than frustrated. "C'mon, idiot!"

My bones rattled in anger as the demon's teeth were all but a lunge away, shouting at its tonsils as they came up to meet me.

"DO IT!" I clattered together, challenging this monster as we erupted out of Hell. I was instantly knocked out. I remember hitting the ceiling hard, being thrown back into the void of its mouth, and instantly dissolving to nothing.

-

Being nothing is a lot like being a blemish on someone's skin; I was not linked with anyone or anything, I wasn't aware of anything. I was, at best, the last few seconds of my life cobbled together into one last, lingering thought.

"How..." The thought started, "... about... that?" How about it? How was that?

I didn't care about anything else. 'How...about that?' My thoughts began to drift apart from each other, mind trying to find peace in its own existence, trying to give that light, silent nod and be happy about what I'd learned.

Happy...   About...   That.

Wait.

About that? Was I happy about that?

No. No, I was not happy about that. Give me five minutes of life and try to instill some sense of fulfillment? Ha! Not happy. Not fulfilled.

I felt myself begin to seep through those thoughts, sinking in as my annoyance gave me a voice again.

"How about... the demon?" The tired, mostly-dead part of me rambled on as I felt myself slowly pulse back to life, slowly realize that I couldn't just let this be done. I didn't like the demon. I wasn't happy about the demon. It was more than a little ridiculous that some stupid, fat-headed demon thought it could just shove me around and take what it wanted. Anger, frustration gave me a very basic mental form, gave power back to my actions. It almost felt like I hadn't been brunch. As I looked around for some demon to strangle, the world suddenly went pitch black.

It felt like I was *somewhere* again. I looked around in this completely dark world before I saw it: a light. Pure white, it seemed to zigzag around in the sky, burning through the world as it tore apart. I followed it, watched it as - just like the demon - it seemed to notice me. The light went absolutely nuts, darting all over the sky before finally stopping above my head. Worried something like before may happen again, I tried to take a few steps away. The light followed.

"I wonder what-" The light suddenly rocketed down, slamming around me like a column of water and catching me in it, screaming out in pain. It felt like little knives were paring me apart, disintegrating me once again as I tried to escape, walls of light solid and impassible. Thrashing back and forth, my fading body suddenly locked up, rigid. A pressure sat on my chest, squeezing the life out of me as my breath became choppy and pained, giving me less and less room to breathe. I swore that'd be the end to this all.

Then, without reason, it let go.

Pupils rattling in my head, my body desperately tried to explain what was going on. Something trickled down my hand: a droplet of water. My eyes darted to my other hand, dripping wet as well. I was entirely soaked, head to soul.

Splatters of color began to apply themselves to the environment around me as it took form, defining the corners of a large room. It was a house, a living room bursting forth from the white light and nothingness. As if watching a negative slowly develop, my eyes darted to the details as they became dark enough to see.

I was... alive?

"What, round two? Haven't we had enough fun yet?" Someone asked tensely, voice low like they were insulted and exhausted - it sounded like a man. My eyes tried to lock onto the figure that spoke up, nothing but a ball of wisps and curves, mostly hollow. A larger man stood behind him, looking vaguely in my direction while he talked with a mother and her child. I pushed my body to make a move, to investigate what they were saying, to try and get a bearing on what had just happened. I was locked in position, immovable. I cringed: the water made it feel like my whole body was on fire.

My jaw was locked tight, unable to move, unable to turn my head or body any position other than how I awoke. I could feel the water on my face and did my best to twitch and shake it off. The first voice spoke again, laughing.

"Aww, does that hurt? It does? Well, good." Struggling to breathe as the man chuckled, I could barely tell he was dancing around like a dolt in front of me. "That's exactly what you deserve for attacking these people here. Demons like you deserve nothing but agony above ground, where you're not wanted."

He laughed, stepping close to my face before delivering a quick, arrogant slap. Confused, frustrated, I coughed out a wheeze of pain - I hadn't done anything. There must've been some mix-up, some... mistake. I began to grow more frustrated, confused and angry. I could see the environment around me now: the couch, the pale sunlight from the windows, what looked to be early morning outside as it stretched across the floor - everything. The only thing left was this violent little ball of annoyance.

"Can..." My voice surprised me, shocked that I was actually able to talk, that I must at least have enough throat enough to communicate. I just wasn't expecting it to be this loud, or this low. Before I could finish my thought, the end of a pole bashed into my teeth, knocking my head back. I whimpered, unable to move, struggling against whatever held me back. Wincing hard, I tried to speak again: "Help... please..."

"After fighting you for a good hour, I'll be dammed if I let you breathe a single word painlessly." I didn't do anything! What was going on? It was right in my face, the bare depressions of eyeholes, or something like them just inches away. Satisfied with this round of torturing, it strode away before turning back to me quickly, something sharp against my throat. My breathing picked up, enduring the lasting pain. The man laughed cruelly again and used the flat of his blade against the side of my face, pressing with just enough force to turn my head. I only breathed harder, mad.

"How does it feel, demon? How's the wrath of the heavens feel on your ragged little soul?" He laughed heartily, pushing my head around and taunting me. If I could groan and roll my eyes at his haughty way of speaking, I would've.

"Not…. me!" I spat out helplessly, boiling with anger and feeling it course through the rest of my body as he teased the blade across my throat. With each new pulse of rage the man took greater form; the shiny, almost-mocking armor adorning him, the pike he held. His eyes were wild and constricted, his stance distanced and ready for battle in various shades of blue and yellow. He was dressed in an ancient medley of attire, like some sort of spiritual warrior crossed with a quarterback with the mockingly bad touch that topped it all off: the feathered wings across his back. I heard the plates of his armor clink as he took a step back, finally, almost contemplating his options. It didn't last long.

The bastard lunged forward with his pike, stabbing it deep into my chest before I could speak again, laughing as he did it. I could feel it pierce through, intensifying the pain I was already in. Clearer and clearer he became with each pulse until he was the same opacity as the people standing behind him, apparently unaware of the butchering taking place. A fighter… angel? I cried out just a bit, a high-pitched whine gurgled into a dull hiss; the sound audible in my ears and the man's as well. He lunged again, making another cut into my neck below my head.

Push! Push! Something urged me on, nagging the edges of my thoughts.

"Your head will make a nice memento, don't you think so?" He laughed again, cutting the pike further into my neck as I could feel it exit behind me, the blade scalding hot. "Maybe I'll stuff it and use it to display my pike."

Internally I screamed, thrashing against the cage this body kept me in. My gurgling became louder, before bubbling at a solid growl. I pushed the boundaries, pulling on my hands with all my might just to make them move; and, like molasses, they began to pull from their position. The weight shifted more to my legs as I grew taller in some respect, both hands shakily jerking up towards my face. My head pulled back farther and farther, lips pulling away to reveal my teeth. The hands in front of my face resembled a humans, though much more calloused and thicker. I watched the streaks of blood-red coloring run down my nose, miles in front of my face and felt the warmth of life reach down to my toes as I was truly born again, snapping back into my control.

The angel stood there, face puckering in concern while trying to take sly steps away. My lungs heaved; my body pulsed with energy, the searing pain of whatever liquid had been dumped on me evaporated away. I could feel my anger rise to the peak of what I had known and surge past it, driving me into insanity. How dare he? How dare he do this?! Wasn't he listening? My weight shifted back to something behind me, standing taller and taller, high above this insignificant waste of dust with his face held in fear, eyes widening as he got a better grasp on his weapon. My growling escalated, throwing my head back and bellowing out a shaking, earth-tearing roar that ensured everyone in a one-mile radius, dead or alive, heard it.

Throwing my weight to the ground, I leapt at the man - only to see the coward already running away from me. He looked over his shoulder and stretched out his gait, darting through the solid wall in front of us. With little thought, I tore through it in hot pursuit, bursting the physical wall as well. Splinters of wood and drywall exploded in front of me into a bedroom, the angel darting through another wall as I followed after him the same way. He skidded on the floor and made a hard right as my debris tumbled behind him, a rolled up pair of socks and bits of a lamp crashing onto the wooden floor alongside. There was no one else in sight. I couldn't see the difference between a mother and a blender; all I knew was my need to tear apart this cocky angel who had the gall to try and sever my head for some stupid novelty.

All was rage as I lunged closer to him, reaching out and swatting the man off his footing with one hand. His clunky, medieval-period shoes scratched the surface of the floor up, stumbling and missing a step before he finally slammed to the ground shoulder-first, a tangle of metal and flesh as he rolled to a stop. I was atop the bastard in an instant, heart racing, seething with unbridled hatred. My two hands grabbed hold of his shoulder armor and pinned him down. I grinned and gripped him tighter, claws penetrating into his skin, denting his armor; he was my prey! I foamed and twitched in diabolical glee, breathing heavily. The angel turned to me, eyes wide in fear, two deep blue pools of terror I knew very well. Everything suddenly stopped, the floor beneath me seeming to drop out.

Those eyes.

They were the only thing I knew very well.

They were blue. Plenty of people have blue eyes, but something lit up in my brain like 'Yes! There you go! You found them! Good job!'

The lightbulb finally went on.

Cold, shaking, I coughed nothing but short heaves. No way. He continued to stare at me, eyes swirling with confusion after a moment as he looked to both of my arms pinning him down, then back to my face. I was suddenly very aware of my surroundings, very aware of what I had done, aware that I was not the only person here. The armor was shining, reflective, but a russet-colored stain in my direction tarnished its glow. As I moved, the stain moved with me, an unidentified mass of red and white. I looked to the two meaty hands grasping the angel; they were not mine.

I dropped the man instantly, scooting backwards until I suddenly hit a wall. Gasping for air that just wouldn't come, I accidentally nudged a cabinet and ran into a fridge before wedging myself there, hands splayed out. Noticing they definitely weren't human, I turned one over, slowly flexing and grasping it. This was me. This was in my control. But what was I?

I shot back to the angel, just now picking himself off the floor - he wasn't injured. He jumped back against the cabinets as I came close. Both of us froze for a moment, generally afraid of the other. Still in mid-panic, I managed to reach out, grabbing his weapon half-embedded into a cabinet. My body awkwardly hopped to the wall and propped the pike up, backing away from it to see the best reflection of myself that I could. Strewn with my blood, the blade gave a distorted picture of a long, red-and-white reptilian face. Slowly, I pulled my lip up to expose the serrated teeth that lined my mouth and the horns jutting from the back of my jaw. My eyes, wild and green, were all but tiny things compared to the rest of me. Craning my head around, I could see a sort of slinky red-and-white body with a strip of hair along its spine, 'my' feet toddling to keep up the position I held now. The tail above twitched with extreme nervousness all on its own.

"Oh… God…" I froze in place, brows furrowed at this whole situation. The angel kept his position against the wall, looking to the other man - a priest as I could see now - as he surveyed the damage I had done. The hallways behind me were practically dripping with shards of drywall, picture frames smashed and bent inward, floor covered in deep grooves. The only thing my mind could hold was a sputtering line of 'what did you do'.

I had done this. ONLY I had done this. This was my fault.

Staring in terror as reality hit me, I sat down heavily, utterly confused and overcome by everything. I wanted to apologize. I wanted to run away. I wanted to go back to being a drifting skeleton in the parade once more; anything but where I was, what I had done, and what I had become. With a glittering sound the angel was behind me, hand just about reaching the pike, eyes fully intent on me. Our glances locked once more, another tremble by the exact blue eyes I had been looking for - the only ones I knew of. They obviously didn't know me. I looked away.

"Are you the police?" I rambled half-heartedly, looking to the priest and the mother slowly picking up bits of wall. "Can…can you tell them I'm sorry? I don't care if I leave or go back, I… oh… shit. I am so sorry." I tried to hold my head, feeling my arms were too short. The angel circled in front of me slowly like he was catching a stray cat.

"I don't think I'm supposed to be here. I don't know how I got out. I don't know how I survived that… or what that was… or… "I vaguely tried to grab at my mouth in some sort of shock. What had I done?

I rocked shakily to my feet, taking a step towards the two people I assumed owned this house, trying to talk to the mother standing there. But her eyes were focused on the damage and nothing else. Tracking, thinking. I was dead. I had to

be dead. The priest suddenly said a quick word to the angel, and him responding in kind, both very nervous. What an awful mess I made. A thought hit me.

"Please, if you can just tell them I'm sorr-"

"Shut up." He hissed at me very matter-of-factly as I shut my mouth. "Can't you see you're not wanted here? Don't you stupid things understand doing shit like this is wrong?"

"I didn't mean anything; I'm not even sure why I'm here. You can talk to the priest, ri—"

The pike leveled at me, covered in golden powder along the whole blade.

"I told you to shut up. Don't you understand what I'm saying?" He leaned in closer, lip curling back, "SHUT." He pantomimed closing a door, before giving me the middle finger and pointing to the ceiling.

"UP. Got it?" When I didn't reply to him, he continued on, "Humans here no like you. Demons bad."

He pointed to the mother and her child, then waved his finger in front of them. I lowered my head a little bit, ashamed. I wasn't sure my intentions were getting through to him. I had no issues with sitting quietly, gaze to the ground.

"God, you stupid monsters." He stood up again, frustrated with me. The angel took a few steps away, muttering to himself before holding a hand over the blade and chanting something foreign. I wasn't sure what he was going to do; I figured that he'd be chasing me back to Hell, back to where I apparently belonged in some hideous demon body I didn't own. I wasn't anywhere as big as that earlier monstrosity, but I certainly wasn't small.

Looking to the mother, I noticed the child around her feet, staring directly at me. It wasn't staring past me, it wasn't looking out the window I sat in front of; it looked *at* me. The child was all of four years old, five at the max, but the kid had a death grip stare on my face. I slowly moved my head to the left, watching her eyes follow, and repeated it to the right with the same results.

"Usually," the angel behind me spoke up, pike resting on his shoulder, "with demons that escape that realm, we send them back where they came from and call it a day. We don't eliminate masses of your numbers; you don't eliminate masses of ours. Keeps everything happy." I kept my head low, scolded. Fine.

"This has been *so* much fun. Not that I wouldn't *love* doing this again, but we're just going to clean everything up right now and make sure you're gone for good." He switched positions on the handle, raising it high over his head, stretching back and chanting again as it glowed a brilliant golden color.

"Waaait wait wait wait a second! I'm sorry, I'm sorry! I'll go back!" I stumbled, darting back into the living room and tripping over my new body awkwardly. Maybe I'd be able to find a hole, a portal, something to get me out of this. My reptilian / human hands grabbed at the carpet, a metal clanking duly resounding behind me. Before I had time to say something, to turn over and plead my case, the angel struck.

The pike tore through my body like I was made of glass, burning red hot on my shoulder down to the small of my back as I exploded into a cloud of black smoke. My remnants shot like a bullet downward, though the floorboards, through the basement ground and back towards the bowels of Hell.

3

"It's here; I know that damn thing is still here." The angel's voice strained with frustration; far away, swimming in echoes and muted through glass - I could hear it as my senses returned to me. I felt my body wedged into something solid, expecting brimstone and deviousness to be my environment now. Instead I opened my eyes to a world of wet, dark earth, but not Hell. Confused, I tried to turn over and get my bearings, finding myself completely encased in the ground like I was buried and laid to rest.

"So, we're NOT giving them peace of mind? Are you saying I'll be going back on my guarantee here, Raziel? They paid good money for that." A different voice, deeper - the priest, probably. Guarantee? The ground knocked louder than the conversation before there was an annoyed grumble.

"I'm not saying that. But I wouldn't be surprised if we've got to make another house call here in a few months. We can blame another spirit then, for Christ's sake; they live next to a graveyard. That's something people believe, right?" The ground thumped much louder as something was thrown against it. The angel complained again, "The hell are you? I know you're in there!"

I tensed up a little, trying to keep extra still; not that I could move anyways. The priest's tone rose quickly.

"If we're trying to convince them their house isn't haunted any longer, it'd be a good idea if you could stop banging on the walls like the damn demon!" There was softer, more muted talking as the angel rambled on his own.

"It's between right here..." I heard some sort of scratching mark, dulled by the earth, "and right... here."

Something shot into the soil not inches from the side of my face, retracted back out of the wall before I could even react. Breathing faster, I prayed he wouldn't do that again. Might've been a little dull with his friendly banter, but he seemed to make a much better demon detector. The other man suddenly spoke up again, louder.

"Stop putting holes in the wall!" He muttered disapointedly like he was angry with a child as the other voice groaned, frustrated. "What failed us? You doubt my ability, or yours?"

"That… thing wasn't phased by my strongest attacks, or the seal. Egh… I mean, that's my high-class stuff there! Holy water made the damn thing change colors!" I could hear metal scraping the floor, the voice getting farther away. "Let them know the house has been purified, give them our number if they're terrified by anything else. I give it a month, max."

Softer mumbling before the sound left all together, heavy feet clomping up the stairs until the door finally shut - I let out a breath of gravel-y air. Twenty minutes passed before there was a slam of car doors above me, the rattle of some kind of engine before all was quiet.

Slowly, I tried wriggling around, going nowhere. Anxious and frustrated, I tried to flop around with no improvement. It didn't make any sense. If I was dead, and I was moderately certain that I was, why couldn't I drift easily through things as the angel -"Raziel" apparently - could?

I thought dead. Thought passable and light. My body shifted a few inches.

Slowly, tirelessly, I wormed my way in a dance-like shimmy through the soil until my nose hit the rough concrete wall of the house. With one last empty thought I broke through, getting an errant hand to the basement floor.

With another ten minutes of shimmying and pulling, I flopped on the ground in beautiful freedom and took sweet, long, beautiful breaths.

I felt awful, slow, and lumbering. Hindered by muscle and size - with barely more than a second glance, I could tell I was still in the demon body. There was no other voice in my head, no driving panic to run away, or to figure out what was, was. I was very large. I was very uncoordinated. I was very burnt out by whatever-the-hell that ordeal was earlier, and the last thing on my mind was to run around in glee. I sat and sulked instead.

I didn't want to be in Hell. It's not a place I dreamed of returning to; but it felt wrong to be here. Felt wrong to be 'alive', like I had been smuggled out of jail, like I had fallen out of an assembly line. I wanted to earn that freedom.

There was a dank ball cap lying on the floor in front of me, a pile of bluish clothes off to the left and various earthy colored garments off a distance in the dark. Light pierced into the basement in a few places; underneath the door jam and through the small windows at the top of the wall. My vision obscured; the giant ball of a nose in my view interrupted a moment of serene peace. My sight was nearly halved; the long reptilian-like nose still jutted from my face, each eye desperately trying to overlap one another in some decent vision. I huffed, tilting my head and snorting in frustration as I whipped around in annoyance, like someone had put an orange between my eyes. Behind me was a mark, a large triangle almost burned into the wall, three outlying marks from each point on it on the exact spot the angel shot me at to try and 'kill me off anyways'. My lip curled at the thought of him.

I rocked to my feet, the unbalanced animalistic ankles instantly crumpling off to the side. It took nothing to throw me back on my butt, my tail whipping around and slapping against one of the wooden supports like a drum. The sound rung out like an awful bell, resonating as I tried frantically to stop it. I froze, steps quickly rushing above me. I felt like I was in trouble; the basement was penetrated by light, the door slamming open as a figure stood in front of it.

"For God's sake, what now?!" She stomped down the stairs in a rush to the basement. The woman from before, the mother, scanned the darkness quickly before throwing on the lights. I scrambled to the other side of the basement with a mix of front and back feet under the cover of darkness, afraid to be seen. She stood at the bottom of the steps, young, black hair, sweatpants; the look on her face said it all. She was unhappy, unnerved, at wit's end. Waves of guilt hit me, ashamed of being such a burden and trouble to these people. It wasn't their fault; it wasn't anyone's, really. But the best thing for me to do would be leave and give them a little rest, let them know I had my wits. That I wasn't going to hurt them. Maybe I could give them that peace now.

I stepped slowly into the light in front of the mother, head hung low. She instantly turned in my direction, squinting into the darkness and took another step down, leaning against the rail cautiously.

"Hiuhhhh." I garbled, before clearing my throat and trying again, "Hi."

She seemed to look expectantly at me, waiting for something. In a rush, I managed to throw together an apology fairly quickly.

"I'm not sure if you can hear me, don't know if it matters." I looked to my toes, all four sets of them, dragging a claw along the concrete nervously. I hated this. I hated this all. The circumstances, the guilt, this whole ghostly experience was surprisingly not a lot of fun. "I'm sorry if I terrorized you; sorry if anyone got hurt. I made a mess of everything, and I can apologize until I'm blue in the face, but-"

"EEEEHHHHHHH!" The washing machine went off, sending me into the air. I leapt, crashing down on a laundry basket that crumpled under my weight, shooting it directly at the wall. The woman screamed, making me scream, the two of us harmonizing for a second before we simultaneously bolted up the stairs. Being the faster of the two I darted to the top, all four legs splayed out in panic.

Not a second later the woman burst through me, through my body without any difficulty, shutting the door which passed through as well. I grasped at my chest, feeling like my spine had been pulled out and had danced around on its own when people and doors passed through it.

"That was not alright." I spat out, trying to regain my composure and get a grasp on the situation. The woman scrambled about the house, picking up her daughter and grabbing the phone; business card in hand. I darted to the couch, sitting behind it as she stared angrily at the basement door, waiting for the person on the other end to pick up.

"Yeah. Hey. It's Katherine, from the house you just said was all purified and free of whatever the hell just threw a laundry basket at my wall? Yeah? Mm-hmm?" The angel! No no no - anything but him. I don't think I could survive another visit. I panicked to intervene.

"Woah, hey! Heeey!" I spoke calmly to the lady, resting my front portion on the couch. She ignored me altogether, so I spoke louder. "HEY! WAIT!"

She continued to look at the door and speak quickly to the priest on the phone. I needed to get her attention somehow and prove I wasn't a problem anymore. At least so I wouldn't have to go through the pain and attempted decapitation like earlier. Next to her now, I spoke like you would to a deaf grandmother.

"HEY! YOU!" Even next to her ear, she didn't hear it. I tried for broke, yelling at the top of my lungs. "HEY!"

She stopped, eyes wide and bewildered, head thrashing side to side before cradling the phone in both hands. The child slipped down to the floor, grabbing onto her mother carefully. She stared at me and smiled, waving. I just stared back.

"Did you hear that!?" I could hear the priest babbling something on the other end. No doubt the angel was probably there as well. "I... I just heard something, like a squeak."

She looked around some more, looking down at the kid, still waving at me.

"Yes, hi honey."

I leaned back on my haunches, confused. A squeak? It was pretty obvious that she didn't get my apology; that the stares, the looks, the ironic placement of herself looking in my direction meant that she couldn't see me, and unless I went around screaming like a spoiled brat, she couldn't hear me either.

"Here, let me put the phone to the air, see if you can hear it too." She put the receiver far in front of her, looking around paranoid in the meantime. Anxiously I ran up to it, putting my reptilian ear to the phone.

"Listen you little shit!" It was the angel's voice on the other end, the sound of the phone changing hands. "I know you can hear me! I know it's you!"

"What kind of sick asshole tries to cut someone's head off?" I gave a furious sneer at the receiver, still angry, unsure how to accurately describe what happened. "I would've gone back myself if I only kne-" The angel cut me off.

"Don't you dare think this is over!" His tone cut up sharply, I could tell he was wringing the phone in his fussy little mits as I only squinted, insulted that I couldn't even get a word in. "Don't think you've won!"

"W-Won? What could I possibly win? Surviving? Why, what are you going to do? Come back and dump some more soda on me?" The woman pulled the phone away, not hearing any more sound from the living room. She began talking to the priest about ways to keep me trapped in the basement. I wasn't through with the angel, though.

"You annoying... angel... man! I don't even know what to call any of this!" I threw up my giant, meaty hands as I could hear some sort of angry response on his end, the mother stopping her conversation suddenly.

"Do you have a static problem on your end or something?" I laughed as she said it, sitting down in front of her. "I need you to come out here and stick to your guarantee and ACTUALLY get this thing out of my house."

I cringed a little bit, breaking my good mood. I was still squatting in this house, and I was still scaring the hell out of innocent people. Amidst the game of death, I had forgotten about that for a moment.

"What do you mean!? I'm not paying another 1300 dollars for you to do the job you should've done in the first place! You promised no ghosts, spirits, or whatever the hell has been haunting my laundry machine for at least six months, and it's only been a week since you 'exorcised' it. Best in town my ass!" She got quiet, rubbing her temples, placing the receiver on her cheek as she took some deep breaths. I took a slow step backwards, resting back like a true animal, ashamed that she might as well be yelling at me.

"Is there anything I can do that's cheap? Mmhmm…mmhmm." She jotted down a few things; something about candles, salt, incense before I grew annoyed and looked away. I picked myself off the floor and walked on all fours towards the wall.

A week. Something that felt like 5 minutes was a week. I grumbled, disgusted with the exorcist combo. If my spotty, Swiss cheese-of-a-memory served me correctly the way a broken puzzle could, a cleansing or blessing on a house was supposed to be provided by the church if you baked them some food or something in return. Not give them a ridiculous amount like 1300 dollars. The mother's voice escalated again over the phone before she slammed the receiver down. I looked back on the family, knowing plainly that I wasn't welcome here as the woman stormed away, frumping down on the couch with a dissatisfied huff.

"Thank you for having me, but I'll be on my way." I pulled together something of a smile, my teeth jutting out from various spots on my lips while the tongue in my mouth, without purpose, dangled out the front; it was a terrible smile. Fortunately, no one could see it. Although the little girl continued to wave at me every time I made eye contact, questioning if I was really invisible to everyone.

Bereft of it all, I turned to the outside wall.

"Bunch of weird people here." I muttered under my breath, shaking my head.

I slowly merged to and through the living room wall to the outside world. The skies burst forth in a beautiful sunshine, birds chirping, gravestones… sitting there, an expansive sprawl of land that if turned the right direction away from the graveyards, was incredible. I closed my eyes and took in a deep breath of air, choking on it for a moment. Something was very wrong here. Standing perfectly still I took in the environment, my heart sagging as it hit me.

The wind; I couldn't feel it. The sun? I could see it, but not feel the warmth. The smell was the same as the house as it was in the ground. The senses I could see, but couldn't interact with. Taking a few steps, my enthusiasm began to dwindle as I moved no grass, and made no footsteps.

Yet here I was busting through walls and jumping on laundry baskets. None of it made a lick of sense.

My head drooped; I didn't seem to have a difficult time with the fact I was dead; more than that, people couldn't see and hear me, save the other supernatural beings on my same level. I felt crushed, lifeless, almost that the world didn't exist with me. I could hear the birds and I could see the wind, but it felt like I sat inside a glass cube, unable to feel the world. It scared me more than anything.

Something ruptured in me for a moment, a slip of panic. I ran full tilt the way a four-legged animal/demon/dinosaur thing should, stretching out farther and farther to get away from the house. The adrenaline, the power, the wild feeling of freedom almost compensated for the lack of connection I had to the world. I looked to the sky, beautiful as it had ever been, clouds skating across a new morning, the world spinning and twirling like it came to greet me.

I began to grin, finally enjoying myself when I slapped hard against the ground in a dead stop.

Dazed, looking around for the person or thing that interrupted my attempt at tranquility, I found no one in sight. Slowly, confused, I tried to take another step away, my left back ankle snagging in mid-air with a sickening jolt. I turned to it, finding my ankles both chained, a link coming out between my Achilles heel and the bones in my foot.

"Ohhh no." I tried taking another desperate step, seeing the links rise up, coasting back towards the house like I had been roped and staked down. My eyes bugged out in my head. "No no nononono."

I pulled harder, more frantic, throwing myself at the barrier that pushed me to the ground again and again. I dug into the dirt, angrier and angrier with my situation, tearing up the grass at the edge of my range, throwing myself against the links. I was stuck here? For some reason, the thought never crossed my mind. I just figured I'd walk out and wander around, experience things, not getting trapped here. Not getting tied to this house.

"Dammit!" I shouted, pulling to the left and making a large arc; chains whirring as they swept over the top of the grass. I put all my force into it, madly intent on either pulling away from the house, or pulling off my feet and being unable to walk any longer. Gritting hard, I pulled and wept for inches of gain, wept for any movement at all before the chains snapped me back, still tethered like any other wandering spirit. No!

With unbridled frustration I yelled to the air. The call swept out in a low, haunting sound.

4

I spent that day outside, broken, disheartened, a heaping pile in the field. Did my best to ignore the massive graveyard next to me and the mound of dirt with the grass seeds sprinkled over it where some big, dumb idiot of a demon came bursting out of the ground. I didn't look around much, mostly cringed at how long my nose was, cringed at the stubby-ness of my demonic fingers. Stupid, vain things like that; made it easier to ignore the big questions.

There was a gratuitous amount of sulking involved, self-loathing at what I was forced to be, self-regret for being stuck with the people I hurt. I could tell it was a stupid thing to do, that of all things to care about, worrying about what I had no control of was pointless. But it still sat on the back of my mind.

I could fix it; the thought rang in my head and pulled my shredded will together enough to sit up and drag myself off the ground. The sun was low in the sky, the tall trees on the rim of the forest casting shadows across the field like loose, poignant prison bars. I could fix it. All was not lost, yet. I could at least try.

With an annoyed groan I got to my feet, watching my arms and legs move in a somewhat rhythmic manner. I began to walk slowly around the yard, my tail flopping about, my body bulky and tense. It felt like I was walking on my hands and knees, like I was scooting about the field, only faster, more natural. Getting the hang of movement, I began a trot, before breaking into a run, consciously aware of how I was doing it instead of relying on panic and intuition. This form was apparently here to stay, and if nothing else, I should be comfortable in it.

I loped closer to the house until the graveyard was practically underneath me, feeling awkward and unwanted in my natural environment as I immediately stopped. It was an expansive thing, headstones dotting the hill, a few people walking solemnly through it on the far side. The rising shadows behind me began to pull over the graveyard, wind briskly howling through the trees.

With a slow, melodic walk, I started into the graveyard, eyes to the pile of loose dirt in the middle. It was between four graves, dirt smattered farther than the mound, like something explosive happened there. It made no sense in my head, nothing did. How did I manage to gain control of this form, when I was sure that there was nothing left to hold onto? The eyes, the angel's blue eyes, had been the only thing on my mind, while all remnants of me were dissolving away. Why was that angel the only thing I could remember? He obviously didn't know me from anywhere, unless a shower of burning pain was his way of saying hello. I felt less panicked; with more memories taking up space, I was more at ease. Worst come to worst, I guess I could find the angel and ask questions another time.

The mound of dirt was spread before me, orange netting covering the whole thing. There were also a few tiny yellow flags to the sides of it, sprouting like menacing weeds in the cemetery. I spread the dirt around with one of my oversized fingers, no call from the mound. There was no Hell, no pull to go back, no sense from it whatsoever, no voice screaming at me to dive underground. Calculating where I'd be least likely to disturb the dead, I drove one hand into the dirt, reaching around like I could snag the top of those caverns. Nothing. It was a mound. It was partially covered in new grass. There was nothing else.

"Suppose there's no going back." I spoke to no one, looking around for some clues. The grave closest to the pile read, 'Anthony P. Settigan' and his wife, 'Susan', with the opposite marker being, 'Samuel Robinton' and his wife 'Rebecca'. None of them were me. I didn't know me, but I feel I'd know myself, given the chance. But these four people, none of them were me. I snorted, frustrated, watching the sun slip below the horizon. The last group of people packed up, their car driving past the mound and me, heading out towards the cemetery's exit.

Overwhelmed by the loneliness of the now vacant graveyard, I sauntered back towards the house, thinking empty thoughts and slipped inside.

It was a bizarre sight. Salt was poured over the threshold; red candles lit around the house and placed along gashes in the wall like little shrines. Or like the power was out. Some kind of weird plant hung in each room and the whole place stunk. I could actually smell it.

"What… the…" I walked delicately through the kitchen, careful not to step on anything placed around the room. The whole house was slightly misty, almost murky, like something was burning in sacrifice. The smell made my eyes water, and made the air sickly and uncomfortable. Light flickered across the linoleum, the shadows from the candles danced along the broken walls. Salt line after salt line seasoned each room, leading to the mother and her child, jumbled and paranoid on the couch, cross in hand. I stopped, guilt-stricken. They were trying to ward me away, trying to keep me out of the house. With all the wall-busting and laundry-hopping, I didn't blame them. Looking at the salt line I batted it with my hand, scattering their decoration across the kitchen floor. They both looked up, the child fussing to pull herself from the mother's grip as she spotted my approach.

"We don't want you in here!" The mother shouted at the corners of the room, like she was chewing out the TV for doing nothing productive. "You've caused us enough trouble!" The mother looked around for any sign of me, readjusting her grip on the child. She hissed out something urgent as the kid rolled and struggled to get away.

"Yes sweetie, I know you're fussy, but your nighties are downstairs in the dryer and mommy wasn't thinking when she went to the store earlier." She spoke back up for me to hear, tone harsh.

"We just want to you to leave. Please." Her voice turned joking, almost sarcastic, "I bet the exorcism probably didn't feel too great. If you leave, then we won't make the priest come back and hurt you." I walked farther into the room, salt tumbling along my path as I noticed something on the coffee table. A box, its tiny wheels moving inside recorded our conversation; with a start she reached across the table and slapped it off, rewinding and playing it. It was a tape of empty air, of slight sounds, of the kid bubbling with spit and gentle rustling.

They were trying to listen for me, but they were absolutely petrified. The way I had acted; at least the parts I could actually be conscious for; it made sense. To them, it would make sense to take all precautions, to do everything in your own power. But I was harmless... essentially. There was no part of me boiling in revenge, no part that wished anything but to just sit around peacefully; not drive a poor woman and her kid over the edge. I certainly didn't need the priest and his angel pal back around here, not right away. I had to make this right. I wanted to have a place to stay. I didn't care if we were best friends, I just didn't want them to be afraid of me anymore. I wanted to convince them that I wasn't evil.

Determined, I loped through the basement door and down the stairs, grabbing the laundry hamper and dragging it behind me. Stopping in front of the dryer, I fumbled to open the door, grinning and ready to try and take back my reputation. I was not a bad person... err, spirit, and I was hell-bent on proving that.

Twenty minutes later, I knocked on the top of the stairs door. Softly at first; I didn't want to scare them.

The woman screamed anyways. I persistently kept knocking, slowly getting louder and louder and probably making it worse. I had no clue how to peacefully introduce the idea of some nonphysical ghost helping out with chores. There's no manual for that.

"Go away! Oh, please, just go away!"

Her high-pitched wailing began to escalate. I poked my head through the door to see her completely paralyzed in fear. She was curled up into a ball on the couch, her child wedged at a weird angle as she screamed into the couch cushions. Frustrated and scared myself, I opened the door, shoved the

laundry basket full of folded clothes through it, and slammed it shut. The mom screamed; louder than before, the wailing began to get softer and softer as she peeked an eye out from her hair.

The screaming stopped abruptly; the woman sat up quickly from the couch, confused, looking around like someone had played a joke on her. She whispered things to herself, too soft to hear, venturing closer to the basket of clothes, all nice and folded. Her face was drained of color, still held with fervent fear as she stood from the couch. The child slid from her grasp, immediately running over to me.

"Hello doggie!" She stood in front of me, arms over her head like she wanted me to pick her up. I looked back and forth; maybe I had been sitting in front of a dog picture, maybe I was in front of her favorite game, but no, there was nothing else. The woman seemed more capable than teaching her child that the door was called doggie.

"Doggie? Honey, what are you…" She trailed off, reaching to the pile of clothes and quickly filing through them, starting to get a grasp on the situation. I sat there, extremely awkward. "Did… uh… Doggie… fold these clothes?" Cautiously, the mother also looked in my direction. I remained silent, feeling the panic rising in my stomach, reassuring myself that they were trying to explain things, to just stick around. The toddler kept her hands lifted up, hopping around on the floor over the salt lines.

"Mmmm hmm!" She hopped over to the clothes, pulling a few out and throwing them behind her until she got to a specific outfit she wanted. The mother reached out and grabbed her daughter by the hand, keeping her close.

"Did you fold these clothes?" She spoke loudly to the house again. There was a very long, drawn out pause, waiting for the house to answer back.

I couldn't answer, so I sat there and felt stupid.

"C-Could you fold those clothes there?" She pointed to the clothes on the ground in front of me, the ones that the kid threw behind her. It was a pair of shorts and a shirt. I eased off my haunches and sat next to the coffee table, folding the pair of shorts easily and scooting them in the mother's direction. She picked them up gingerly, wiggling them like they were possessed by the Devil himself, like they'd get up and dance around.

Something unexpected happened - she giggled. She laughed, or more accurately, gagged on air. I relaxed too, letting out a deep sigh.

"Are… uh… are you a good ghost?" She kept her eyes fixated on the shorts while I folded the shirt. I pushed them to her side of the table. The woman jumped, seeing the folded shirt and began to laugh more in disbelief. "I take that as a yes. Good God, my house is possessed with the spirit of a maid!"

She rocked to her feet, abandoning her kid to stand by the table alone, kicking line after line of salt away as she trudged into the kitchen.

"I… I need a drink… or… a lobotomy. Maybe I'll just slam my head in the car door a few times." She pulled something from the cabinet over the fridge, suddenly shouting my direction. "Good ghosts don't bust holes in my new house, you son of a bitch!"

She laughed as she said it, like it was all one big joke - something like 'Ohhh hoho, you crazy demon!' I sighed and hung my head low, some mix of guilt and relief. The kid was at my feet, looking up at me, continuously waving.

"What's wrong Doggie?" She tilted her head and smiled as she caught my attention. I frowned, a little bewildered.

"You can't honestly see me, can you? Did your mom drop you on your head as a baby or something?" I joked, leaning farther away from her. The kid kept staring straight at me, suddenly throwing her head back and yelling to her mother.

"Moooooom, did you ever drop me on my head?!" I froze in terror. The kid giggled as her mother emerged with a red-hot glare from the other side of the partition to the kitchen. She suddenly began stomping in my direction while I tried to gather that I actually had a person who could relay messages. Sure, she was some four-to-five years old, but apparently I was accepted, understood, by a five-year-old. I just assumed I couldn't speak to anyone.

"Tell your mom that Doggie was joking!" I nudged the kid as she kept her eyes to her mother. "You know, ha-ha, funny joke?"

"Ha-ha!" The kid repeated, probably the most pointless part of the message. The mother was back in the living room now, pinning me backwards with an impressive amount of blind accuracy. I wasn't in the mood to have my soul danced around in; it sure didn't feel like fun the first time.

"I... uh... I'm sorry!" The mother kept coming, footsteps pushing closer. I forgot I needed to crank my volume to twelve to be heard. "SORRY!" I belted out, back against the wall - the mother stopped dead in her tracks, glass of wine in her hands. She looked up to the corners of the wall, then back to the kid, then back where I essentially 'was'.

"Says sorry." The toddler spoke out, rummaging through the clothes. The mother nodded her head slightly, completely confused.

"Yeah..." She seemed to withdraw into herself a bit, turning back to the couch. With haste, she snatched up the recorder on the table, rewinding it back in a sense of awe. "I heard it too, sweetie." I remained hunched down, body braced for impact; staring back and forth for a conclusion of some sort to be reached. The mother pressed the recorder to her ear intently - the sound of the previous conversation came through, remarking about the ghost-maid and the slow trailing words that the mother needed medical help.

I leaned forward and listened with them, suddenly feeling the full weight of what was going on here. I was dead. Very dead. That, for some reason, still hadn't hit me, but hearing my own distorted, distant shout sound nothing but a scratchy whisper really drove it home. It was odd, seeing people trying to connect with me, that I wasn't in their same existence, that I was on some other level. It all just hit me.

I sat very hard, heart heavily sinking in my chest. My hands began to shake as I couldn't support myself anymore, slumping to the ground. The kid came up next to me and sat by my head, stroking my imaginary hair like she meant it. Pity from a five-year-old. I closed my eyes and wished I could disappear, too lazy to push her away.

"What's wrong, honey?" The mom stopped the recorder and set it down.

"It's sad." She kept stroking my 'hair', her hand passing through me in fairly uncomfortable waves.

"Why is it sad?" The mom came over to my side of the table; I opened my eyes to see her looking over me as well. Pity. I groaned and closed myself off again.

"I dunno." The kid kept petting me the way any child pets an annoyed animal; with a lot of unnecessary force. A thump; the mom placed something next to my head, wood floors creaking as she eased back and sat on her feet.

"You're the talkative one, you tell us." She spoke directly at me, where her daughters hand was. I stared up at the woman from the floor; her look actually seemed to be on me, not on the table, not on the couch, not distantly far away in paranoia. On me. I switched to the tape recorder in front of me, blowing some air at it. "C'mon, what happened, lost your nerve? I'm not hearing anything, Doggie."

There was the tail-end of a sneer, trying to goad me on. Considering the circumstances it made me smile, or grin at least. This woman was quick to overcome her screaming, tearful paranoia to challenge me straight on. It was refreshingly ballsy.

"Why am I sad?" I spoke with my lips to the recorder, tone not shy of someone yelling at a deaf old man. "I'm stuck. I can't leave."

The mother snatched up the recorder in a heartbeat, already rewinding it back and boosting the sound as she walked to the couch. I pulled myself from the floor, walking calmly to her side to try and hear it as well. The tape crackled with static, with the drastically loud thump of being set on the ground. A few seconds of shuffling, before my voice spoke through, so softly.

"...sad?" It sounded garbled, like I'd eaten the thing and spit it out before finishing my answer, "...stuck. I can't leave." They were clear. Feminine too, not like I sounded to myself at all. It was soft like a person muttering it from a house and a half away, but I could hear them; I wasn't that close to the recorder. The mother stared at the machine in her hands and almost dropped it onto the coffee table, setting it down and pressing the record button.

"Are you just tricking us? Are you that same... thing... that attacked us before?" She stared at the spot I had been on the floor.

"No. Not exactly - I don't think." I stopped, worried that my garbled sentence was going to come out wrong, "If I was, I'm good now. No more of that." I laughed nervously before the mother grabbed the recorder again, listening to the chunks of words able to get through. 'Not exactly', and 'I'm good now', with an evil, foreboding laugh attached to the end of it. I groaned, frustrated.

"Good now? And we find you folding laundry. What am I supposed to make of this?" She posed the question without the tape recorder on. I shrugged regardless of documented sound as the mother put her recorder on the table. She receded back into herself, sitting farther away on couch. "Well. So now we have a laundry-folding ghost in our new house. I guess we were asking for it, living next to a cemetery." She laughed and rubbed the bridge of her nose.

I eyed the tape recorder, figuring I could make this work better.

Smacking the red record button, I startled the mother and her kid, pulling it closer to me so I could shout from a more comfortable distance.

"I'm sorry. I don't know what I'm doing, or why I'm here." I stopped, pushing myself to annunciate the best I could with a long, pebbly demon mouth, "What's your name?"

Shutting the recorder off, I rewound it and tilted it towards them. This time, my voice came out at something of a normal tone, like a regular whisper. But it all came out; every word. The mother slowly tucked her legs back underneath her in a sort of bemusement/bewilderment combo, looking to the little girl, then back to the recorder.

"It… its Katherine. Katherine Faegel." She laughed after she said it, leaning to her daughter, "This is Amber… um… what's your name?" She began nervously scratching a part on her leg with a sense of urgency and fear. I turned the recorder back to me.

"I don't have one." I had to work hard to push anything; but I was starting to get a hang of it. It seemed like things around the house only moved at my touch if I was angry, passionate, determined, or any other emotion as far as I could tell now. But lazy, relaxed, or resting actually made things more difficult. With our conversation growing more comfortable, pushing down on the recorder got harder and harder.

Katherine nodded and pulled her child closer, spitting out the real point of this conversation. "Is there anyway we can make you leave? Say a prayer or something?" My stomach dropped again, regret wearing down on me.

"I've been trying to leave all morning. I'm sorry for disturbing you." I turned from the living room to go into the kitchen as my voice spoke from the recorder, more distorted and garbled, like how the interrogation started. I was exhausted. It was near midnight now and I had no more energy to play telephone. I needed rest. I wasn't going anywhere. Things would get sorted out another day.

I walked throughout the house, slowly, things faintly familiar, hazy memories from the demon. I felt stupid and ashamed. What had I done to these people to have them resort to such an expensive exorcism? They seemed level-headed enough, not the type who'd run out and buy such a service on a whim.

Maybe it'd been years. Maybe hundreds of years. Maybe I've been haunting this same plot of land for lifetimes upon lifetimes. If five minutes felt like a week, there was no sense of time to me, at least right now. Everything was uncertain. Unknown. Above all things, I didn't have a name; all I knew about my life was a fight where I chased an angel through some walls, then got my ass handed to me, and blue eyes. Now I could add bargaining with terrified people to my short list of life experiences. Oddly, this didn't seem to help things all that much. I still felt terribly empty, unfulfilled, and being chained to a house wasn't helping much either.

Leaning against the wall, enveloped in shadows from the lightless room, I stared out at the stars in the sky. Familiar. Skewed in some way, but familiar. It was a reassuring sight, calming, silencing. I closed my eyes and imagined feeling the cool wind blow past me, and feeling the land resting.

"I have a proposition for you, ghost." I jumped, startled, finding the mother and her child behind me, the kid pointing exactly where I was like a little blonde bloodhound. "My… daughter will be pointing you out when I need you. But I have a proposition. If you will listen to it, knock on the wall or something."

I looked to the wall behind me, rapping my hand against it.

"Here's my proposition; you don't haunt us or attack us again, and we won't call any more priests or exorcists here." She held up a hand, like she was instructing her invisible daughter. "In turn, you also have to make sure that no other unwanted guests come in here: ghosts, burglars or solicitors. Otherwise I'll have to call a priest and no one wants that."

I slowly began to smile, getting the gist of her intention. She was allowing me to stay on the condition I acted like a guard... demon.

"Lastly, you answer to me. My first command is 'Don't come into my bedroom while I'm sleeping, because it's terrifying and I'm not real adjusted to this yet'. Second is to give me and my daughter some time to adapt to this. Sound okay?" She looked left of where I was sitting, off position from her bloodhound's point. "One knock for no, two knocks for yes."

I leaned back again, rapping twice on the wall. The woman smiled, muttering to her kid and leaving the room awkwardly after a moment of consideration, like she was surprised that I didn't put up more of a fight about her demands. I could hear them enter some other room, softly talking and laughing to one another. It was mostly the mom, Katherine, congratulating her child for doing such a good job. They were an odd family. Not bad, but a little odd.

I smiled a bit more, looking back to the stars and stretching out along the ground. Counting the constellations I could remember, I drifted off into a strangely peaceful sleep in a strange, strange situation.

5

The next two weeks went by uneventfully. Katherine and Amber didn't communicate with me and I mostly kept to myself. Things greatly relaxed between us all; it became a kind of grace period in the household. The space gave me time to really take in my surroundings, to know the people I was 'guarding', and develop a sense of self all over again.

The house was perched on lifts, stilts almost, on the edge of the Juan Julio Cemetery. I had no idea who Juan Julio was, but he was important enough to get his own cemetery, that lucky dog. The Faegels - my landlords so to speak - lived in a practically uninhabited area. There was the cemetery, an abandoned house much farther down the road, and something like a fishing dock farther than that. That was the limit of my vision, the rest of the area was mostly obscured by trees.

I habituated a brown house, the very back end of the second level touched regular ground with the basement acting as the bottom level. The front was held up by thick supports, decoratively disguised to be like modern, sassy pillars so it didn't look like we lived in some shantytown. The garage was partially into the ground as well, a door leading straight into the basement. On the front of the house, overlooking the road, was a long, serene deck that I spent a lot of my time on. It was one of my favorite places to go, slumping around peacefully as I adjusted to my new life.

From time to time I'd patrol the perimeters, sit on the edge of the property alongside the road and watch the cars whiz past. I also got to know the names and dates of my silent audiance in the graveyard. Maybe one of them had importance, I still felt like a fluke and if nothing else, but it kept my mind busy. I felt like I had places to be; restless, needing some sort of actual purpose instead of a implied, thrown-together one.

I grew more used to my form as well. It didn't feel nearly as awkward as it had when I started out. Still weird, but the sensation that I was scooting around on my hands and feet soon fell away. It had a lot of natural bounce to it; a lot of pep and lots of energy. I wasted time racing birds, lapping the yard and bowling over decorations with my house-chain if I could gather enough speed. I managed to keep myself busy in the simplest way, but it did the trick; I came to appreciate the tiniest bit of life I could still enjoy.

The Faegels were interesting people. Katherine left early each day, taking Amber with her to return at about six that evening. There was no husband, no boyfriend, not one that I had met. She was a woman of about thirty-five years old, a smoker; her skin the slightest tinge of grey on an otherwise youthful face. She had dark blonde hair dyed black, a thinner, taller woman, self-dependent. Very laid back, she was altogether a good mother in the most unusual times. Even pushed to the edge of her limits, she managed to bounce back quickly and only taking a few breaks now and then to glare at the house in disbelief, shaking her head.

Amber seemed to be almost five years old, tow-headed, at the age where she was a handful; I'd often see her bolting across the yard after a bug or bird of some sort, occasionally taking her time to stop and wave in my direction before bounding back to her mom. The girl kept an eye on me at all times, more silent as of late after her mother told her it would be best to leave the Doggie alone because it needed rest. I didn't mind a break from the fascinating world of ghost whispering, and neither did Katherine.

On the weekends she spent a lot of time gardening, maintaining a bed of flowers alongside the garage. Amber was always out there with her and they pretty much spent the days doing little things; cleaning, maybe watching a movie, playing outside. It wasn't a flashy life, there weren't box socials or midnight raves going on, just mundane family type of work.

I'd just be there, more or less hanging around, bored out of my wits.

Finally, the vow of silence broke as Katherine talked with Amber at the edge of the yard. They both came towards me as I sprawled out on the grass, half-heartedly sunning myself. I heard them before I saw them, the little girl whispering 'Hi' with each step closer to me, finally stopping just short of where my spirit and the grass intersected. I yawned, stretching out before closing my tired eyes.

"Hello dinosaur!" Amber shouted practically in my ears as I winced in pain. Putting one hand to my head, I rolled away from them.

"I have a name for you." The mother said matter-of-factly, her daughter nodding in agreement. "I mean, only if you want one."

I quickly flopped back on my stomach, nodding rapidly in hopes that the little girl would repeat my answer; she did.

"Alright, good. I actually have a list of them, let's go back into the house and get you a name." She began walking without me as I scrambled to my feet, trotting behind her like I was an actual part of the conversation.

"I appreciate the time to relax, too. I'm not 100% on my house being haunted by maid-ghosts, but you're better than whatever that thing was before." She trailed off as we entered into the building. I couldn't help but feel guilt stricken.

Katherine put Amber down in the middle of the kitchen, quickly walking to the other room to get her name list.

"Watch her if you could, ghost." She said it nonchalantly, just like. 'Hey, goddess of the wind, wash the dishes if you could, please'. I watched after the mom, becoming increasingly aware of the child at my feet.

"Your mother says some odd things. Things that even I find weird." I looked back to the girl, muttering under my breath, "Things that a dinosaur demon-person ghost finds weird, which I guess is an accomplishment." She stood beneath me, unamused, a look in her eyes that demanded I play with her, or she'd be tempted to drink the chemicals under the sink out of boredom.

"Uhh, wanna play Simon says? Kids like that, right?" The girl's frown turned immediately, jumping once in place before taking a few steps back, readying herself.

"I do." She swung her arms at her side, waiting for my first command; I gave a little laugh and stood on all fours, mirroring her. "You go first."

"Alright. Simon saysss… touch your nose!" I pulled my head closer to my stubby arms, touching my nose; the girl did the same, "Alright, good. Simon says pat your head." I lowered my head more to the ground, patting the top of it. I hit something hard, something that was not a part of my body; instantly I froze.

Feeling around the outside of it, I could tell it was a circle, with some sort of rubber strap connecting around my top jaw horn. Following it back to the circle, I felt a bridge over the top of my head, with a similar circle on the other side; it was in a natural dip in my skull, and felt like it was barely there at all.

"Goggles?" I wondered aloud, the mother came back into the room to find her daughter jumping around with her finger on her nose and hand on her head. She looked at us both and laughed, scooping Amber up to sit on her lap.

"I see you two had a game going on, eh? Well, maybe next time Doggie can teach you how to fold laundry, help mommy out with some cheap labor on her chores." She laughed and bounced the girl on her lap, ruffling through the papers scattered about the table. Grumbling slightly, I stood next to her, the kid pointing out exactly where I came to sit.

"Alright, so I was looking through a database of names, what they mean, and where they come from. If any of my suggestions sound good, knock on the table, let me know." She smiled oddly, warmly, like she was trying hard to make

this commonplace and not obnoxiously weird. "You are a woman, I presume?"

I knocked on the table. Based on the recorder, I had to assume so.

She went through the names she liked, one by one, starting with Abigail, Abby, some odder names like A'la'a to names like Kristen, Kady, so on and so forth. Nothing struck me, everything rolled off as I sat there, playing with the goggles on my head. They didn't move. I tried jabbing my finger underneath it, using my tail to try and pry it off, but it held on tight as if it was glued down.

Katherine kept going through the list, the wear obvious in her tone as well. At least she was making an effort to bring me a little comfort, which for the last week I figured she was just hoping I'd leave.

"Nabeela, Nadeen, Nahara, Nao, Nella, Neri, N…"

Bells went off. Whistles, firecrackers, snap-pops; they all went off. It sounded so close, like it hit me over the head with familiarity. I knocked on the table like a drum. Neri. Neri hit a nerve. It was like a burst of light, of energy, of excitement. Agh, yes, there was hope after all!

"Which one, you damn woodpecker?" Katherine spat out. I stopped tapping on the table, prancing around it instead as she read the names off one at a time. When Neri came up again, I knocked on the table and sat, almost proud of myself. It wasn't my actual name, but it sure as hell was close. Close was good.

"Neri." The mother tongued the word carefully, deciding if it stuck or not. "Alright, I can live with that." She leaned over where I sat before and patted the air.

"Means 'My Burning Light'. Fancy." She shuffled her papers as her daughter snickered and looked at me. She was trying, even if it was comforting the air. Katherine sat up in her chair, looking to the empty spot still, "My work is closing down on Thursdays and Fridays now, so we'll be keeping you company here at the house more often. I'm hiring a babysitter those first few weeks, so please don't scare the hell out of her, okay? It's important for me to do my work here, so don't think we'll be playing and romping around all day, Neri."

I stared at the mother for a moment, before giving a knock on the table once more from the opposite side. Her glance switched to my side before looking to her daughter.

"Was mommy talking to nothing for a while, Amber?" She smiled as she said it, the girl giggling in response, before pointing me out. "Anyways, we also have a repair man coming in tomorrow to fix our walls, as well. So, you know, don't scare him either. Don't get me wrong; scare everyone else, but just not those people. Do your best to keep the Jehovah's Witnesses away from my doorstep while you're at it, they've come back with more energy this time." She got up from the table taking Amber with her, leaving me to sit alone in the middle of the kitchen as the glow of receieving a name slowly wore off.

I sat, perfectly still, hearing the fading footsteps, the barely audible birds outside, the house resting. That was it. There you go. This is all I had to look forward to. Silence. That was that; I had a name, that's all there was. My stomach began to slowly knot up, slowly churn on itself, rising to my heart as it began to beat harder. That was the only sound, like a sharp-ticking clock in silence, it only personified how vastly empty this house was; more specifically how alone I was. What more did I have? What more was left? The relaxation was nice, but it wasn't enough to keep me entertained, to keep me happy. The clotted, choking knot wound itself tighter.

This was it. The rest of my life. The rest of everything I had to interact with, a life devoid of conflict; trapped, stuck to this house. I looked around me, looked to my feet, looked at the rhythmic swaying of the branches against the wind as they too stopped. Everything went still. Nothing.

I gagged, suffocating on the silence.

Neri. Well, Neri was going to crack under pressure if something interesting didn't happen in the next ten minutes. I began to breathe hard, searching for something to chew on, something to destroy in an inexpensive way. I left the house, strutting across the field, trying to figure why I felt like this. Maybe all the isolation was finally getting to me? Maybe this is why there were no nice ghosts around - they all just finally snap because they're too bored. It was starting to make sense why they haunted. I personally felt moved to scare the hell out of someone, just for some entertainment. Just for... something. Interaction, excitement - try and avoid figuring out why my soul had been sent to Hell, maybe. Try and ignore that crushing weight on my back.

Without thought, I loped to the trees, feeling that familiar pull on my ankles before I could get there. I growled, leaning against the chains to the point where they hurt. I could still feel that. I wasn't completely dead. I pulled for a while more.

It wasn't enough. Doubling back, I ran full-out to one of the posts supporting the house, trying to bang my head on it. I don't know what I was thinking; I think the finality of this all was driving me a little nutty. No use - my head kept going though the post, no matter how angry I was. I couldn't seem to hurt myself on the 'physical' things I could touch, just grab and manipulate them.

"This really is Hell!" I tried one last time, almost tripping down the hill as I passed through the beam once again. I stared angrily at the post before going back inside, looking around frantically for something to destroy. If only there was something here I could break, something on my level.

Like a pal ghost I could talk to...

Eyes wide, I slowly scanned over to the phone. I could... call the angel. Not to go all buddy-buddy with him but, you know, maybe get some pointers on what I was supposed to do. That wasn't too taboo, was it? I wasn't inviting him over for a drink; I just needed someone to validate my semi-existence.

"Yeah, yeah, keep telling that to yourself." I muttered under my breath, flipping through the cards on the table before I got to the only exorcism card in the bunch.

"Great Beyond. We go to the 'great beyond' of savings." I read flatly, feeling my hope fade already. "Not for 1300 dollars."

I knocked the receiver off the hook, the numbers on the front of the phone. I tried to dial the number on the card, finding my fingers hitting four buttons at once. Pushing it back onto its stand; I tried again, this time using a pencil. It hummed, warbling like static air. I kept what I thought my ear was to the end of it, even finding the dial tone relaxing in some way, before a man briskly picked up the phone - the priest.

"Hello?" He said politely, like he had been waiting for this call. "Hello?" The lump in my throat wrapped around the back of my head, fighting to speak to something; someone.

"Hi! Hello! C-can I speak with the other guy? Your angel pal? Russle… maybe?"

"Hello?" He sounded annoyed, juggling the phone in his hands, "Heelllooo? If this is a prank call, for the last time, this is a real business. Who is this?" I was going to lose them if I didn't do something quick. Panicking, I began to smack the phone on the counter and growled into the receiver before putting it back to my ear.

The priest hesitated, laughing before there was a second voice in the background. The angel!

"Hey, I think your demon pal's on the phone." He chuckled, the phone being turned over to what anyone else would consider dead air.

"Uhh… hello?" He said, fairly calm and confused. I started to sweat a little bit; this was a stupid, stupid idea. Pulling the phone away from my head, I stared at the reciever, worried. What was I doing?

"H-Hi there!" Was all I said, nicely as possible, considering the circumstances. It was all I had to say. He geared up to full crazy in no time flat.

"You have some nerve calling me again!" Barely a pause before he continued on without my response, "What? Call to brag about dragging your shamed soul around for another day? Think that since you managed to cower long enough underground that you've won, you spit?"

"No, no I—"

"If we weren't busy eliminating the rest of your friends, we'd be over there exterminating you from all levels of this planet!" He seethed at the end of his words, too angry to form another sentence and giving me enough time to get a word in.

"I'm not trying to pick a fight, I just want to talk." The growing feeling of guilt and frustration overwhelmed me, too heavy this early in the day. Yeah, it was a bad idea to call.

"Now you think you're such a smartass that you can call me here and hex me, or harass me, or whatever the hell you're doing? God, its cases like yours that make my job all the more necessary, erasing stains like you off this plane of existence for good. God damn you!" The phone switched hands as I heard him storm off, the priest muttering before the phone was hung up.

"Maybe it just wanted to be friends..." He laughed, the phone silencing with a click. I stayed where I sat, frozen still, the deafening silence again bearing down on me. Staring at the holes in the reciever like I could crawl inside and hide there, like something would scramble out, I took a shakey breath and sighed; stupid. Slumping forward, I rested my head on the counter broken, almost. Stupid.

"Wonder if you've got any tips for making the time pass." I muttered dead to the air. "Maybe some insight on how to deal with being something that everyone inherently hates. Or being dead. Not really settled with either."

Sighing, I gently placed the phone back on the counter above my stupidly placed goggles with delicate, monster-sized claws.

Hearing the phone do nothing but growl its monotonous displeasure, I sat like that for some time. Eventually I exited out the back door again, walking silently, downtrodden until I was at the edge of the cemetery.

There I sat until the sun fell below the horizon, thinking everything over. Maybe I was damned to haunt this house, to be completely separated from everything around me. I didn't deserve any special calling, or anything different than any other ghost, I guess. Maybe I should just count my blessings that I can communicate with the two people I live with, stop being so demanding. Maybe that was my place in life.

It felt like I was waiting for something to happen, that I was waiting for excitement to come along. I think my imagination was stretching just a little too far. I didn't want my life to be about habitually fitting in. I wanted... something. Couldn't tell what that was, though.

Crickets chirped in the cemetery before me, the fog slowly rolling in from its northernmost edge. My exit lump of dirt was all but absorbed back into the earth, grass covering the bump like it never happened. Everywhere around me life was telling me that it was moving on while I sat in the same instance I left Hell with; confused, lonely, and frustrated. The graveyard unnerved me before, I never stayed out after dark for fear of whatever monsters had attacked before were just waiting for me. But now, I just hoped that a few other spirits might be around for some conversation.

"Is anyone out there?" I called out to the cemetery, sitting politely on the edge of it. "I'm not looking for a fight, just for some other bored spirit to talk to. There's plenty of you here, right?"

A whole lot of nothing answered back.

"I'm not as mean as I might look, I swear." I said a little quieter, feeling stupid. "I guess you guys don't have a lot of ghosts coming over here to chat, I mean, I don't blame you. If I saw some dinosaur-faced demon sitting and talking to me, the last thing I'd do would be strike up a conversation."

I listened for any sound, any voice. Everything was quiet.

"What am I supposed to do?" I hung my head low, frustrated. "The hell am I doing here…"

Staring at my feet, I wiggled my claws, letting out a heavy breath. The graveyard was muted; it seemed to be filled with nothing but resting bodies, their souls long departed. I sighed again, extinquished and quiet.

"Maybe people are satisfied with little things, they're happy to find a place in life to call thier own, where the tiny changes they make within thier lives make them happy." I scratched the back of my head, flexing my bulbous fingernails out once and away like they disgusted me, "I'd give anything to have just… something happen."

The voice breeding now was young and meek, this spongy, downtrodden version of true emotion, more frustrated than sad.

"I don't think there's anyone here to talk to. Nothing here but a lot of empty bodies and one idiot trying to talk to them."

Slumping to the ground, I shut the world out. A long, frustrated sigh followed

"You can tell me things" I jumped, scanning for the voice, only to find it coming out of Amber standing ten feet behind me. Her mother was farther up the hill, arms crossed.

"She won't go to bed until you go to bed," Katherine smiled, "Neri."

"Why don't you tell me stuff?" The girl squatted closer to me, sitting side by side. I was a little awestruck, babbling on my words out of shock.

"I'm not aiming to burden children." I grinned haphazardly, really hoping I could find another spirit in the middle of a graveyard, of all places as she squinted a little, not getting what I was saying. "You're too little."

"Nuh uh, I'm almost…" She held up one hand, fingers splayed out before double-checking manually. "Five!"

I smiled and nodded politely, looking back to the graveyard.

"Why are you sad? Do you miss your family?" The girl asked honestly, sitting a little closer to me. "Cause I miss my dad sometimes." Head snapping back around to the kid, I frowned, somewhat surprised. I could hear the mother shifting her weight a little, letting out a sigh. Thinking, mulling it over, I readjusted my answers to keep things from going further into the depression pit.

"I do." I lied, I didn't have any idea if I had a family or not. I started to say something more as Amber scooted until she was practically rubbing elbows with me.

"You're very warm." The girl looked up at me, happy and oblivious in the glazed-over way that kids use. They don't care about the big things, they live entirely in that moment. Very blunt, very honest. I smirked.

"Uhh… thanks. That's very kind of you to say." I was a little confused, but let it slide. "What happened to your dad, if you don't mind me asking?"

"He got sick. He's with the angels now. That's what mom says." She looked over the graveyard with me. "But Mom says that death is a in-ev-it-ab-le part of life, that we can't be scared of it." She said it carefully, like she'd rehearsed it in front of a mirror, stumbling over the words. Katherine spoke up from the porch of the house, distantly.

"Well Mom, and Mom's therapist say that." She muttered sarcastically as I gave a quick grin, turning back to Amber.

"I suppose that's very true." I responded, considering the notion. The little girl smiled.

"Are you with the angels too, then?"

"No, I don't think so." I looked back to Katherine, who was busy picking some dirt off the side of her house. "I'm not sure."

"Is that why you and the angel were fighting?" She started picking the blades of grass alongside her before looking up at me.

"You could see him too, eh?" I laughed a little, more tired than anything. "I think we were both just very confused."

"Is that why you're sad?" Because you're confused?" She was hitting these questions with a creepy amount of accuracy for someone her age. Her mom was staring right at her as well; she must know how observant her child was.

"I think I'm a little overwhelmed, while also being a little underwhelmed." I looked back to Amber as she frowned and stumbled on what I meant. Clearing my throat. I started again. "It's a term adults use when they're confused, so you're right, I'm confused." It was just easier to go this way. She suddenly grinned.

"Maybe you and the angel can be friends?"

I laughed out loud at that one, hushing myself so I wasn't belittling the kid.

"I don't think that's going to happen. He's not interested in being friends."

"Why were you were calling his number then?" She giggled back, knowing she had me cornered. I could feel my eyes bug out of my head, at least a little bit. "Did he want to be friends? What did he say?"

"You know, I'm not really sure myself, he seemed pretty mad." I smiled a little, looking back to the star-filled sky. "And no, he was pretty clear on that one."

I watched the child shiver like mad for a second, doing her best not to let that dampen her good time, sitting out near midnight by the cemetery. Shaking my head, I motioned back towards the door.

"I think it's time to go back inside" I grinned, getting up from my spot. We trudged back up the hill, Amber relaying what our conversation had been about while I lumbered alongside, shaking my head. I called because I wanted help.

"Neri, stay alongside me here." Katherine said quieter, then louder for her daughter. "Go on ahead inside honey, mommy's gotta talk with Neri." Amber looked at both of us, opening the back screen door by herself and going inside.

"I know you can't talk back to me, so just listen." The mother spoke tersely. "I don't want you calling that priest anymore, I mean, I thought that was your rule, and here I find you calling him yourself." Her scowl let up for a second, mumbling under her breath that she was talking absolute nonsense. After a moment, she put her hand on her head, pulling back her hair.

"If you're bored, or depressed, or whatever, let me know instead of calling and looking for trouble like that. When I said I was with you, I meant it; that man is nothing but a drain on my finances." Katherine said, "You're bored? I can understand that. I'll get you some puzzles or something in the morning. Sound good? I'll do my best to keep you entertained; you seem like an active thing." The woman laughed, starting to head inside.

"Boy, I guess it's good that my only neighbors are a bunch of dead bodies, I think I'd have child services called on me if people saw me talking to dead air in the backyard all the time." She waved a hand over her shoulder, "C'mon, it's time for bed."

I felt honored. At the very least, more accepted into the tiny family on the hill here, having people consider me like that. That night I curled up on the floor of Amber's bedroom, sleeping heartily with the rest of them like I belonged. Maybe other ghosts haunted because they were stubborn, that they didn't try to fit in. Maybe because they actually missed their families, longed for them, wished for that interaction. As I drifted off to sleep, I wondered what I had done differently.

-

Life was more comfortable after that. The next morning, I awoke to a stack of old puzzles lined up just outside the girl's door, everything from 500 to 5,000 pieces. They were stupid pictures of puppies and three ducks and a ball, but it was entertainment. Eventually, we found other activities for me to do that would keep me entertained; play blocks, little square blocks that I could make spaceships, or castles, or whatever I wanted and finger painting. It was all kiddy stuff, but it was quick, cheap entertainment, and it kept me from feeling like I had to gnaw on the walls to be happy.

I watched over the house as requested and stayed away from the babysitter while she was over. Every now and then, I'd kick a chair just to keep her on her toes, which led to Katherine telling her eventually that the house was haunted by a friendly ghost. It didn't matter; it was the last we saw of her. We got a new babysitter after that, one who liked to rummage through the cabinets looking for money. She was kindly persuaded to leave after I made a doll float after her, judgingly. Our last babysitter was an older woman, Sabina, who even after we told her that the house was haunted with a nice ghost, stayed. She even insisted on leaving a small plate of food out for me at dinner, just so I felt included.

Death was good for a while, things worked out, and everyone benefited. It stayed like that for three wonderful years.

-

Sabina sat in the padded chair, watching TV while Amber and I played with a mix of her Darby dolls and play blocks, what we dubbed 'The Grand Castle Siege on Hollywood'. I waggled the blonde doll at Amber's identical one, ushering a challenge of supreme despair.

"Come, Darby, I challenge thee to a duel! Your Caramel Macchiato against my Vanilla Espresso!" I laughed, shaking the tiny coffee cup in Amber's direction.

"I splash thee with fruity flavorings and a dash of my Claymore!" She posed the tiny sword in Darby's hands, smacking the coffee cup from mine.

"Vile fiend! You've ruined my fifteen hundred dollar purse! Thy lawyers shall be invol-" I shuddered to a stop, feeling the air around me ripple and distort, a large black mass pulsing in the corner. My vision snapped to it instantly as I dropped the doll. The uneasiness crept on my skin.

I slowly got to my feet as the disturbance passed alongside the walls. It channeled through the TV, the screen flickered madly before turning off with a start. It then sharply shot to the farthest wall, leading into the kitchen.

"Neri, what is it?" Amber asked cautiously, still bent down low.

"I'm not really sure. Get your mom, keep everyone in this room, okay?" I tracked the disturbance into the kitchen, the shadowy lump of energy hanging around that corner as well.

"Be careful!" Amber called, darting behind me to go get Katherine.

"I'm always careful." I said absentmindedly, glaring down the mass in the corner. It spiked out as I crept nearer to it, distorting and reforming itself like it didn't know what to do. With a low, haunting sound, it began to laugh; the mass heaving and chuckling as a face came to surface in the black goo. A skull of some animal slowly pushed its way out of the wall, two yellow, pupil-less eyes rolled around to face me as the black, smokey mass dropped to the floor. Taller, taller it got until it towered over me, body forming into one I could barely remember, one that I had never seen myself, but was unmistakable.

"It's been such a long time, my good friend!" The demonic mass chided happily, its head skidding on the ceiling. The monster's eyes rolled around in two channels through its skull, balancing on two heavy front legs and a long, disorganized tail from behind. I started to shake my head back and forth. This… this wasn't possible! The demon seemed to pick up on my confusion. "Had fun on your little excursion out of Hell, huh? Confused? You thought that holy water had gotten rid of me, I get it. Please, I'm not that easy to kill."

I slapped on a quick smile trying to cover my confusion, taking a few steps away from it. What was this thing doing in our house? What did it want from me, or from the rest of my family?

"You're the demon that tore me out of Hell, aren't you?" I spoke bluntly, a little mystified to say the least. Why didn't this thing attack back three years ago after it all happened? Why wait this long?

"Aww, you do remember me! I figure this has been more than enough time to sort your shit out. Ready to go back?" It laughed at my face, a mix of horror and confusion. "Yeah, you're all set; come my queen, it's time to go back now." It gave a royal little bow with its blackened, crumbled bones. I only shook my head harder.

"What? Whose queen?" I glared at the beast, pulling my lip back in a snarl, "I like it here, and I've got no interest in going back to Hell. I am not your queen." The demon gave what could be considered a frown, crouching down lower to the ground.

"You're not going to make this easy, are you?"

"No, I love making life difficult." I grinned, spotting Amber and Katherine out of the corner of my eye. "Stay over there!" I yelled to her, the girl stopping in her tracks. Too late; the demon spotted the two of them, charging in their direction as a broken mass of flesh zipped just by my face. I lunged, grabbing onto the trembling bits of its tail and pulling down hard. Amber screamed, pulling back on her mother as well as the demon's jaws snapped just short of the two women.

"Call the Priest!" I shouted through clenched teeth, gritting and tugging at the demon, "They're the only people that can help deal with something this big, even if the angel is an idiot!"

The demon whipped around with a jarring snarl, roaring out in a challenge as it gathered speed. Dropping the tail end of it, the monster charged straight into me, pressed tight against the wall. I couldn't go through it! More, more pressure as it tried to smother me, tried to encase me in that horrible black mass. Something cracked; a snap, the wall held as long as it could before the demon suddenly punched a giant hole out of the kitchen to the outside world.

I tumbled head over tail far into the field, hoping that the sunlight would kill the hulking black mass emerging from the house. It roared, lurching forward, doubling over with a second set of arms growing out where a set of legs should be. Scrambling to my feet I tried to face it, the two of us circling around one another, snarling. My thoughts were only of my terrified family inside.

You can find the rest of the novel online at caelum-sky.tumblr.com